Gramma's
STORIES & RHYMES
for
Little Christians

Written by Margaret A. Lang

Illustrated by Linda Giggee Smith
Garretson, South Dakota

SPECIAL RECOGNITION

FIRST EDITION

ISBN 0-942242-00-9

Printed in the United States of America

Published by Lang Publications
490 North 31st Street - Suite 100
Billings, Montana 59101

Distributed by:

World Bible Publishers
Iowa Falls, Iowa 50126

PREFACE

My children being grown with children of their own, I now realize what a precious charge the LORD gives each time a child is born. I understand why JESUS said, "Suffer little children to come unto me, and forbid them not: for of such is the kingdom of GOD." Matthew 19:14, and what He meant when He said, "Except ye be converted, and become as little children, ye shall not enter into the kingdom of heaven." Matthew 18:3. Many come upon this understanding far too late in life - some never do. It is for this reason that I have such a burden for children everywhere.

I was therefore impressed to write this book for, and about children. How they think - how they feel - the things they do - how they relate to GOD. To help them to understand how GOD loves and cares for them, and has made it possible for each of them to become a child of GOD through faith in His son JESUS CHRIST (Gal. 3:26). It is important for children to learn at an early age that GOD hears and answers the prayers of those who believe and pray in JESUS' name (Matthew 21:22 and John 14:13), and that all things are possible with Him (Mark 10:27).

If, when you read this book, you will take the time to look up and read all the references at the end of many of the poems herein, it will be a great help and blessing to you and to those being read to. "So shall my word be that goeth forth out of my mouth: it shall not return unto me void, but it shall accomplish that which I please, and shall prosper in the thing whereto I sent it." Isaiah 55:11.

"Train up a child in the way he should go; and when he is old, he will not depart from it." Proverbs 22:6, "If any of you lack wisdom, let him ask of GOD, that giveth to all men liberally and upbraideth not; and it shall be given him." James 1:5.

May GOD bless the children,

Margaret A. Lang

THE LORD'S PRAYER

Our father which art in heaven, hallowed be thy name.

Thy kingdom come, thy will be done in earth, as it is in heaven.

Give us this day our daily bread,

And forgive us our debts, as we forgive our debtors.

And lead us not into temptation, but deliver us from evil: For thine is the kingdom, and the power, and the glory, forever. Amen.

Matthew 6:9-13

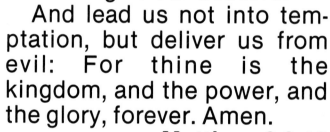

THIS BOOK IS DEDICATED TO:

My children and grandchildren who are my inspiration.

My husband—who is my help and encouragement.

My GOD—who gave me the ability and opportunity to write this book.

MY PRAYER:

That children everywhere will be brought to a saving knowledge of our LORD and Saviour JESUS CHRIST.
Matthew 19:14

INDEX

INDEX, continued

RHYMES Continued - - -

PSALM 150

1. PRAISE ye the LORD. Praise GOD in his sanctuary; praise him in the firmament of his power.

2. Praise him for his mighty acts: praise him according to his excellent greatness.

3. Praise him with the sound of the trumpet: praise him with the psaltery and harp.

4. Praise him with the timbrel and dance: praise him with stringed instruments and organs.

5. Praise him upon the loud cymbals: praise him upon the high sounding cymbals.

6. Let every thing that hath breath praise the LORD. Praise ye the LORD.

GROWING WITH GOD

GOD LEFT SMALL GIFTS OF LOVE WITH US,
  AND IT'S SO NICE TO HAVE THEM NEAR.
THEY'RE PRETTY TO LOOK AT, FUNNY SOMETIMES,
  AND ALWAYS DELIGHTFUL TO HEAR.

SOON THEY'LL GROW UP TO BE BIG,
  THEY'RE ONLY LITTLE AS YET, YOU KNOW,
THEY'VE MUCH TO LEARN IN EVERY WAY,
  AND I'LL HELP THEM AS THEY GROW.

I'LL TALK TO THEM OF GOD'S LOVE FOR US,
  AND TEACH THEM HOW TO PRAY.
AND ALWAYS MY PRAYERS WILL FOLLOW THEM,
  AS THEY GO ALONG LIFE'S WAY.

MARY PONESSA

BED TIME

Two little children
  ready for bed,
Climbed up on Grandmother's
  lap and said,
"Please tell us a story,
  Grandma dear,
And sing the song
  that we love to hear."

Grandmother told them
  the stories true,
How little David,
  the giant slew,
The fiery furnace
  and three brave men,
And of Daniel in
  the lion's den.

Though they had heard
  the stories before,
They were glad to hear
  them all once more.
Then Grandmother sang,
  "Jesus Loves Me",
To the two children
  upon her knee.

SOON THEY WERE YAWNING
  AND NODDING THEIR HEAD,
SO GRANDMOTHER TOLD THEM,
  "IT'S TIME FOR BED."
SHE TOOK THEM TO
  THEIR ROOM UPSTAIRS,
AND LISTENED TO
  THE CHILDREN'S PRAYERS.

"JESUS BLESS MOMMIE
  AND DADDY TOO,
BLESS RAGGY DOLL,
  AND WINNIE THE POOH.
BLESS GRANDMA, GRANDPA
  AND MITZE AGAIN.
THANK YOU, JESUS,
  GOOD NIGHT AND AMEN".

"GOOD NIGHT, PRECIOUS ONES",
  GRANDMOTHER SAID.
THEY HUGGED HER NECK
  AND JUMPED INTO BED.
TUCKING THE COVERS
  AROUND THEM TIGHT,
SHE KISSED THEM BOTH
  THEN TURNED OUT THE LIGHT.

11

JUST PRETEND

I HAD A SHIP I SAILED TO SEA,
WHEN I WAS TWO, BUT ALMOST THREE.
I SAILED IT TO THE WORLD'S END,
BUT IT WAS ONLY JUST PRETEND.

SPRING FUN

OH WHAT FUN IT IS TO PLAY
  IN PUDDLES IN THE SPRING,
TO TOSS A LITTLE ROCK IN,
  AND WATCH IT MAKE A RING.

TO TAKE YOUR SHOES AND SOX OFF,
  (MOST EVERY CHILD KNOWS,)
AND FEEL THE SOFT WARM MUD,
  GO SQUISH BETWEEN YOUR TOES.

SCHATZE (SHOT-ZE)

SCHATZE WAS A TINY DOG,
  (THOUGH HE THOUGHT HE WAS BIG).
HE CHASED THE STRAY DOGS FROM HIS YARD,
  AND BARKED AT THE NEIGHBOR'S PIG.

HE MADE SURE THE SQUIRRELS AND BIRDS,
  STAYED OUT OF HIS YARD TOO.
AND WHEN THE YELLOW KITTY CAME,
  HE KNEW JUST WHAT TO DO.

THEN EARLY ONE BRIGHT MORNING,
  SCHATZE FOUND, OUT BY THE WOOD,
A KITTY OF ANOTHER COLOR,
  AND IT DIDN'T SMELL SO GOOD.

HE CHASED AFTER THE KITTY,
  AND BEFORE SCHATZE COULD THINK,
THE KITTY SPRAYED HIM WITH SOMETHING,
  THAT SURE DID MAKE SCHATZE STINK.

13

DOES JESUS CARE?

DOES JESUS REALLY CARE
  'BOUT A CHILD SMALL AS I?
OR IS HE MUCH TOO BUSY,
  TO HEAR ME WHEN I CRY?

DOES JESUS REALLY LISTEN
  WHEN I CALL TO HIM IN PRAYER,
AND TELL HIM ALL MY TROUBLES,
  DOES JESUS REALLY CARE?

YES, JESUS REALLY CARES
  'BOUT CHILDREN EVERYWHERE.
WHETHER YOU ARE BIG OR SMALL,
  HE'LL LISTEN TO YOUR PRAYER.

WHETHER YOU ARE BLACK OR WHITE,
  OR YELLOW, RED, OR BROWN,
WHETHER YOU LIVE IN CITY,
  IN THE COUNTRY, OR SMALL TOWN.

JESUS IS NOT TOO BUSY
  TO HEAR EACH WORD YOU SAY,
HE CARES ABOUT YOUR TROUBLES,
  AND LOVES TO HEAR YOU PRAY.

HE CARES SO MUCH ABOUT YOU,
  I'VE OFTEN HEARD IT SAID,
HE EVEN KNOWS THE NUMBERS,
  OF THE HAIRS UPON YOUR HEAD.

Luke 12:7

JESUS CARES

TAKE YOUR TROUBLES TO JESUS.
MENTION THEM IN YOUR PRAYERS.
NO PROBLEM IS TOO GREAT OR SMALL,
FOR JESUS REALLY CARES.

Casting all your cares upon Him! For He cares for you. **1 Peter 5:7.**

COOPERATION?

TWO LITTLE BOYS
   WENT OUT TO PLAY
ONE BRIGHT SUNNY
   SUMMER DAY.

JIM HAD A BALL
   LEE HAD A BAT.
(TELL ME, WHAT DO
   YOU THINK OF THAT?)

LEE SAID TO JIM,
   "PITCH ME THE BALL."
JIM ANSWERED HIM,
   "NO! NOT AT ALL!"

SO EACH BOY WENT
   THEIR SEPARATE WAY,
AND NEITHER ONE
   HAD FUN THAT DAY.

TWO LITTLE GIRLS
   WENT OUT FOR FUN,
BENEATH THE WARM
   SEPTEMBER SUN.

ROSANNE HAD JACKS
   JANE HAD A BALL.
(I DON'T THINK THAT'S
   STRANGE AT ALL.)

JANE SAID, "COME ON,
   LET'S PLAY A GAME."
ROSANNE WANTED
   TO DO THE SAME.

SO THE TWO GIRLS
   STARTED TO PLAY,
AND THEY HAD LOTS
   OF FUN THAT DAY.

Prov. 3:13

15

THE SAND-BOX

To her little sand-box,
  One warm summer day,
With her pail and shovel,
  Annah went to play.

First she built a castle,
  Built it strong and tall,
Next she made a sand-man,
  By the castle wall.

Then along came Herbie,
  Herbie was her cat,
Walking in the sand where,
  Little Annah sat.

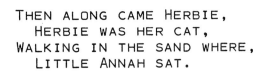

He knocked down the castle,
  And the sand-man too,
But Annah didn't mind,
  She could make them anew.

16

BE KIND

BE KIND TO ALL GOD'S CREATURES.
  NEVER HURT A LIVING THING.
FOR GOD MADE EVERY ONE OF THEM,
  AND LIFE TO THEM DID BRING.

SPEAK SOFTLY TO THE KITTEN.
  PLEASE DON'T HURT THE NEIGHBOR'S DOG.
FEED THE LITTLE BIRDS IN WINTER,
  FOR THEY ALL BELONG TO GOD.

LET THE TINY LADYBUG,
  FLY, FLY, AWAY BACK HOME.
LEAVE THE FUZZY CATERPILLAR,
  TO WANDER WHERE HE MAY ROAM.

YOU MUST REMEMBER ONE THING,
  IT IS VERY OFTEN SAID,
THAT EACH GOOD, OR BAD, DEED YOU DO,
  COMES BACK ON YOUR OWN HEAD.

EPH. 6:8   PSALM 7:16

17

A NEW FRIEND

Wayne watched out the window as the new neighbors unloaded the moving van next door. "Boy! What old furniture they have, and look at that old lamp. They must really be poor."

Just then he noticed a young boy about his age helping his mother unload the family car. "Patches on his jeans," Wayne noted, "and he walks funny - I suppose he'll expect me to be his friend and show him around school just because I live next door to him."

Wayne stayed out of sight the rest of that day. The next day was teachers convention so Wayne hurried off to the park to ice skate with his friend Jeff. "You should see my new neighbor," Wayne said, "He limps and wears patches. I hope he doesn't expect me to be his friend."

"Well, just ignore him," Jeff said, "that's the only way to handle that."
At noon the boys hurried home for lunch. Mother was just putting it on the table when Wayne came in the door. "Wash your hands, Dear, lunch is ready."

Wayne washed up and sat down at the table. They all joined hands, and bowed their heads to pray. Mother asked the blessing and in conclusion added, "And bless Mrs. Anderson next door, LORD, you know she's going to need a lot of help since her husband has been ill so long." They all said Amen and began to eat their lunch.

After lunch Wayne left for the park again, hoping Jeff would meet him there. It was such a nice warm day, he was glad there wasn't any school. Jeff wasn't at the park yet but Wayne was sure he would be along shortly, so he put on his skates and began to skate around the pond.

Wayne hadn't realized that the warm sun had melted the ice and made it thin. Before he knew what was happening, he heard a loud "CRACK." The ice broke and Wayne was in the icy water.

"HELP!" he shouted, trying to hang on to a chunk of ice. The water was cold and deep. "HELP!" he shouted again. Water had gotten in his eyes and he could hardly see.

"Here, grab this stick." A strange voice called. Wayne reached out and got a hold of the stick. The boy on the bank pulled him ashore. Wayne recognized him as his new neighbor. The boy gave Wayne his warm dry coat and carried Wayne's wet one as they hurried home to dry off and change clothes.

Later that day Wayne went over to the neighbors to get acquainted and thank his new friend for saving him from the icy water. "Hi, I'm Wayne," he introduced himself, "What's your name?"

"Andrew Anderson," the boy replied, "but my friends call me Andy."

"Welcome to Westfield," Wayne said, "and thank you for your help this afternoon. I'll walk to school with you in the morning and show you around."

"Great," said Andy, "Mom usually goes with me on the first day at a new school but she can't leave Dad. Dad and I were in an accident a few months ago. He's getting better and may be able to go back to work in another month. My leg is getting better too. The doctor said it is only a matter of time and I won't even be able to tell it was broken."

The boys were together the rest of the evening getting acquainted. Wayne discovered Andy was an "O.K." guy and felt quite guilty for his bad attitudes earlier.

That night as Father read the Bible to the family before bed, he read, "Judge not and you will not be judged. Condemn not and you will not be condemned. Forgive and you will be forgiven." Luke 6:37.

Wayne had learned his lesson. As the family prayed together, he silently prayed, "LORD, forgive me for my wrong thoughts and actions toward Andy. And thank you for sending him my way. Amen." Then he climbed into bed and quickly fell asleep. He had had a big day.

19

JANUARY'S WHITE WITH SNOW.
AREN'T YOU GLAD GOD MADE IT SO?

FEBRUARY IS SO COLD,
TO PLAY OUTDOORS, ONE MUST BE BOLD.

MARCH WINDS THAW THE FROZEN GROUND
CROCUSES BLOOM ALL AROUND.

APRIL RAINS AND GENTLE BREEZE
AND BLOSSOMS ON THE APPLE TREES.

IN MAY THE GARDEN WE WILL SOW,
GOD WILL CAUSE THE SEEDS TO GROW.

JUNE IS HERALDED WITH A SHOUT,
HURRAH! HURRAH! SCHOOL IS OUT!

20

JULY — THANK GOD FOR SUN AND RAIN,
WHICH HELPS TO GROW THE SUMMER GRAIN.

IN AUGUST, IT'S A GENERAL RULE,
CHILDREN GO TO BIBLE SCHOOL.

OCTOBER FROST AND EARLY FREEZE —
COLORED LEAVES FALL FROM THE TREES.

WARM SEPTEMBER DAYS ARE FUN.
HARVEST OF CROPS HAS BEGUN.

NOVEMBER — WE GIVE GOD OUR PRAISE,
FOR BLESSING US THESE MANY DAYS.

DECEMBER — LET US EVERYONE,
THANK GOD FOR HIS BLESSED SON.

21

BE A LITTER BIT CONSIDERATE

BEFORE YOU THROW SOME LITTER DOWN,
  PLEASE STOP AND THINK A BIT.
ISN'T THERE A BETTER PLACE,
  YOU CAN DEPOSIT IT?

CONSIDER FOR A MOMENT,
  IF OTHERS DO LIKE YOU,
HOW MUCH LITTER WOULD THERE BE,
  TO CLUTTER UP THE VIEW?

NOT ONLY IS IT UGLY,
  BUT IT COULD HARM SOMEONE.
STEPPING ON SOME BROKEN GLASS,
  IS CERTAINLY NO FUN.

NOW WE COULD DO MUCH BETTER,
  IF INSTEAD OF THROWING DOWN,
WE WOULD PICK SOME LITTER UP,
  AND HELP CLEAN-UP THE TOWN.

IF EACH ONE WOULD DO HIS PART,
  IN KEEPING GOD'S WORLD CLEAN,
THERE'D BE NO MORE LITTER,
  ANYWHERE, TO BE SEEN.

Psalm 24:1

THE BIG SURPRISE

WHEN SHE WAS LITTLE, KARI LYNN,
GOT INTO THE FLOUR BIN,
SHE WAS GOING TO MAKE SOME PIES,
FOR HER MOMMIE A SURPRISE.

SHE PUT SOME FLOUR IN A PAN,
AND ADDED WATER THEN BEGAN,
TO STIR IT SWIFTLY WITH A SPOON,
WHILE FLOUR WENT FLYING 'ROUND THE ROOM.

SHE HAD SOME FLOUR IN HER HAIR,
ON THE FLOOR AND EVERYWHERE,
NOW KARI LYNN WAS QUITE A MESS,
WITH FLOUR EVEN ON HER DRESS.

MOMMIE CAME IN AND BLINKED HER EYES,
KARI LYNN CALLED OUT, "SURPRISE."
YES, MOMMIE WAS SURPRISED IT'S TRUE,
AND KARI LYNN WAS SURPRISED TOO.

23

STOP THE SWING

WHEN I WAS SWINGING
   EVER SO HIGH,
I COULD ALMOST REACH
   UP TO THE SKY.
I COULD LOOK ACROSS
   TO THE NEIGHBOR'S YARD,
REACH THE TREE-TOP
   IF I TRIED REAL HARD.

MITZE SAT AT THE
   FOOT OF THE TREE,
LOOKING BACK AND FORTH
   AS SHE WATCHED ME.
I THOUGHT HER NECK
   WOULD SURELY TIRE,
OF WATCHING ME
   AS I WENT HIGHER.

I STRETCHED MY FEET
   TO REACH THE CLOUD.
MITZE STARTED
   TO BARK REAL LOUD,
TO TELL ME WHAT
   SHE WANTED TO SAY,
"PLEASE STOP THE SWING,
   COME DOWN AND PLAY."

DIZZY DUKE

DUKE IS A LITTLE WIENER HOUND.
HE ISN'T TOO SMART - IS HE?
HE CHASES HIS OWN TAIL AROUND,
'TIL HE BECOMES QUITE DIZZY.

MORE BLESSED TO GIVE

Patty was feeling pretty big as she walked into the department store with a whole dollar in her pocket. Mother had given her the dollar to buy Christmas gifts for her four sisters and brother.

Because Father had gone to be with JESUS the Christmas before, the family was very poor, yet somehow Mother had managed to give each of the children a dollar for their Christmas shopping.

Patty walked down the aisle that was filled with toys, and came to the section where all the dolls were on display. Being not quite five years old and not having a doll of her own, she quite forgot the real reason she was there.

"Oh," she thought, as she picked up a pretty rubber doll, "This is the nicest dollie I ever did see. And look, it even has a bottle. It only costs ninety-eight cents. I have just enough money to buy it." Quickly she took the doll and the dollar to the counter and paid the clerk.

With her two pennies change in her pocket and the doll in her arms, she skipped happily down the walk toward home.

But as she got closer and closer to home, her feelings of happiness began to disappear. "Oh my!" she said aloud, "now I won't be able to buy gifts for the other kids."

Patty realized at once what she must do. She ran back to the store as fast as her little legs could go and told the clerk she had changed her mind about the doll. The clerk returned her money and Patty began to shop for something nice for the others.

Ribbons for the twins, hair clips for Nayoma, paper dolls for June and color book for Leon - "I have 20 cents left," she thought to herself as she counted her change. "I know! I'll get something for Mother." Carefully she looked at everything in the store then finally decided to get the pretty little pot-holder with the daisies on it.

Patty's heart was happy as she placed the neatly wrapped gifts under the tree. She knew this would be a nice Christmas for everyone. And it was - especially for Patty. For she had learned it is more blessed to give than to receive. Acts 20:35.

GOOD MORNING, GOD

GOOD MORNING, GOD.
   WHAT A NICE DAY.
I'M SO HAPPY
   THAT I CAN PLAY.

I THANK YOU THAT
   I'M WELL AND STRONG,
I WILL SERVE YOU
   ALL DAY LONG.

BY HELPING MOM
   AND MINDING DAD.
BY BEING GOOD
   INSTEAD OF BAD.

BY BEING KIND
   AND COURTEOUS TOO,
I'LL BE MORE
   AND MORE LIKE YOU.

Psalm 5:3

BED PARTNERS

I SLEEP WITH LITTLE SISTER,
AND HER BIG RAGGY DOLL,
WITH HER CAT AND TEDDY BEAR,
THOUGH I DON'T MIND AT ALL.

BUT WHEN SHE HAS THE BED SO FULL,
FROM THE FOOT UNTO THE HEAD —
AS SOON AS I AM FAST ASLEEP,
SHE CROWDS ME OUT OF BED. Eph. 4:32

28

THE WIND

"WHERE DOES THE WIND BLOW?"
    ASKED THE LITTLE GIRL,
AS SHE WATCHED THE GOLDEN LEAVES,
    TAKE OFF IN A WHIRL.

"DOES IT GO INTO THE TREES,
    THERE TO SPEND THE NIGHT,
OR RUSH BEHIND THE BUILDINGS,
    IN FAST AND FURIOUS FLIGHT?"

THOUGH WE CANNOT ALWAYS KNOW,
    THE ANSWER TO HER QUERY,
WE DO KNOW GOD IS IN CONTROL.
    THEREFORE, WE DON'T WORRY.

Matt. 8:26-27

29

HIDE AND SEEK

A GENTLE BREEZE WAS BLOWING,
  SOFTLY IN THE NIGHT.
CHILDREN PLAYING 'HIDE-N-SEEK',
  BY THE PALE MOON LIGHT.

JASON COUNTED QUICKLY.
  THE OTHERS RAN TO HIDE.
TAMMY HID BEHIND THE TREE,
  AND BRENDA WENT INSIDE.

KEVIN THOUGHT HE'D PLAY A JOKE,
  AND GOT THE OLD BEAR-SKIN.
HE HID BEHIND THE CELLAR DOOR,
  AND WAITED WITH A GRIN.

WHEN JASON WENT TO FIND HIM,
  HE JUMPED OUT WITH A ROAR,
BUT HE WAS MUCH MORE FRIGHTENED,
  THAN JASON WAS, BY FAR.

MATT. 7:12

THE FAMILY OF GOD

I LIVE IN A HAPPY HOUSE,
 ON THE CORNER OF PLEASANT STREET,
AND THE FOLKS WHO LIVE HERE WITH ME,
 ARE THE NICEST YOU'LL EVER MEET.

WE HAVE JOY* AND PEACE* IN OUR HEARTS,
 AND MUCH LOVE*, ONE FOR THE OTHER,
LONGSUFFERING*, GENTLENESS* AND FAITH*,
 PROVOKING NOT, ONE ANOTHER.

FOR WE'RE A PART OF GOD'S FAMILY.
 ANGRY WORDS ARE NEVER SPOKEN.
NO ONE HERE EVER GETS UPSET,
 WHEN SOMETHING IS SPILLED OR BROKEN.

EVERY WEEK WE PUT ON OUR BEST,
 AND GO TO THE CHURCH OF OUR CHOICE.
THE ONE THAT'S ON SALVATION ROAD,
 WHERE WE SING AND PRAY AND REJOICE.

Gal. 5:22 *FRUITS OF THE SPIRIT

WEEKEND AT THE FARM

I CAME TO THE FARM FOR THE WEEKEND,
  TO VISIT MY UNCLE AND AUNT.
I'D LIKE TO SPEND THIS WHOLE WEEK HERE,
  BUT MY DADDY TOLD ME I CAN'T.

I HELPED MILK THE COWS THIS MORNING,
  AND RODE ON THE HORSE UNTIL NOON.
I FED THE PIGS FOR UNCLE VIC,
  AND GATHERED THE EGGS FOR AUNT JUNE.

I KNEW THAT I'D HAVE LOTS OF FUN HERE,
  FOR THERE'S ALWAYS PLENTY TO DO,
BUT BEFORE I COULD SAY "JACK ROBINS,"
  THE WEEKEND WAS OVER AND THROUGH.

OH - I ALMOST FORGOT TO TELL YOU,
  BEFORE I ENDED THIS POEM,
THAT MOMMA DOG HAS FIVE PUPPIES,
  AND I MAY TAKE ONE OF THEM HOME.

GOD ANSWERS PRAYER

THE POOR KITTY CAT,
  IN THE WINDOW SAT,
WITH HIS NOSE PRESSED TO THE PANE.
HE TRIED TO MEW,
  BUT HE HAD THE FLU.
HE WANTED IN, OUT OF THE RAIN.

HE LOOKED A SIGHT,
  BUT I KNEW HIS PLIGHT,
SO I HURRIED TO LET HIM INSIDE.
WHEN I BROUGHT HIM IN,
  HE WAS SOAKED TO THE SKIN,
SO I TOWELED HIM 'TIL HE WAS DRIED.

HE ATE MILK AND BREAD,
  AND I PUT HIM TO BED,
THEN I PRAYED FOR KITTY THAT NIGHT.
I'M HAPPY TO SAY,
  HE WAS BETTER NEXT DAY,
AND HIS EYES WERE SPARKLING AND BRIGHT.

Mark 11:24   1 John 5:14

33

HIKING AND EXPLORING

WE WENT HIKING IN THE HILLS,
JUST DIXIE DOG AND I.
WE TRAMPLED OVER ROCKS AND RILLS,
UNTIL THE EVEN WAS NIGH.

AND WHEN WE WENT EXPLORING
THE CAVES OUT SOUTH OF TOWN,
I BROUGHT SO MANY TREASURES HOME,
THEY ALMOST WEIGHED ME DOWN.

AUTUMN LEAVES

WHEN AUTUMN LEAVES ARE RED AND GOLD,
  AND FALLING ALL AROUND,
I LIKE TO RUN AND PLAY IN THEM,
  AND HEAR THEIR RUSTLING SOUND.

WHEN AUTUMN LEAVES ARE ON THE GROUND,
  AND BALMY BREEZES BLOW,
WE RAKE THEM ALL INTO A MOUND,
  AND WATCH THE FIRES GLOW.

THE SECRET OF HAPPINESS

ERIK WAS A HAPPY BOY,
  AS EVERYONE COULD SEE,
ALL DAY LONG HE SANG A SONG,
  OR WHISTLED MERRILY.

SOON OTHER CHILDREN WONDERED,
  WHAT MADE HIM SING WITH GLEE?
WHY DID HE ALWAYS WHISTLE?
  WHAT COULD HIS SECRET BE?

THEN ONE DAY HE TOLD THEM WHY,
  HE WAS A HAPPY BOY.
"IF YOU LOVE JESUS MOST OF ALL,
  HE'LL FILL YOUR HEART WITH JOY."

Psalm 7:17

OH! OH!

JIM WAS WATCHING DAD WASH THE CAR,
AND OFFERED TO HOLD THE HOSE.
AS HE TURNED TO SEE A BUMBLE BEE,
HE SPRAYED POOR DAD IN THE NOSE.

DANDELIONS

MY MOMMIE LOVES DANDELIONS.
  I KNOW, 'CAUSE SHE TOLD ME SO.
SHE PUTS THEM IN HER NICEST VASE,
  AND PLACES THEM WHERE THEY SHOW.

POP-CORN

MOTHER'S MAKING POP-CORN
  IN A PRETTY PAN.
SIS AND I ARE TRYING,
  TO HELP HER ALL WE CAN.

I PULL UP THE STEP-STOOL,
  SO I CAN REACH THE BOWLS.
SISTER GETS THE BUTTER,
  AND SHAKER FULL OF HOLES.

SOON THE SMELL OF POP-CORN,
  AND BUTTER FILL THE AIR.
THERE ISN'T ANY OTHER,
  FRAGRANCE TO COMPARE.

AS WE EAT OUR POP-CORN,
  AROUND THE FIRE BRIGHT,
FATHER READS THE BIBLE,
  BEFORE WE SAY GOOD-NIGHT.

Prov. 22:6

MR. SNOW-MAN

ONCE I BUILT A SNOW-MAN,
  BIG AND ROUND AND FAT,
I PUT SISTER'S SCARF ON HIM,
  AND DADDY'S SUMMER HAT.

THEN WENT BROTHER'S GLASSES,
  ON HIS CARROT NOSE,
A ROW OF SHINY BUTTONS,
  FROM HIS CHIN DOWN TO HIS TOES.

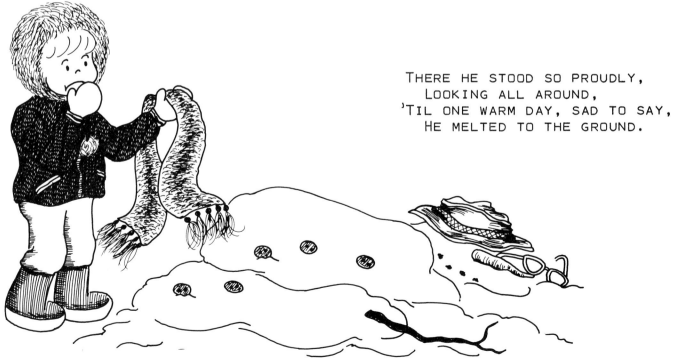

THERE HE STOOD SO PROUDLY,
  LOOKING ALL AROUND,
'TIL ONE WARM DAY, SAD TO SAY,
  HE MELTED TO THE GROUND.

A GIFT FOR MOTHER

The two girls stood in front of the store window reading the sign that read, "MOTHER'S DAY - May 9th." "Oh, I don't have any money for a Mother's Day gift," Linda said. "I'll have to think of some way to make some money before Sunday."

"Maybe you can get a job or find some pop bottles and sell them." Joy said, "I have a dollar I've been saving from my birthday money. I saw a pretty box of hankies at Bergum's store, I think I'll get for Mother."

The girls walked down the street toward home. They said goodby at the corner and Linda ran the last half block to her house. She could smell the apple pie before she opened the door. "Hi, Mom, I'm home," she called, putting her books on the couch.

"I'm in the kitchen," Mother called back.

"Mom, do we have any pop bottles you want to get rid of?" Linda asked, as she came into the kitchen.

"No, Dear, why do you ask?" Mother replied.

"Oh - I just wondered." said Linda. She changed her clothes and started outside to play.

"Linda," Mother said, "Will you please take the apple peelings out and throw them over the fence for the horse?"

After some grumbling, Linda did as she was asked.

Later that week on the way home from school, Linda said to Joy, "I still don't have enough money to buy a Mother's Day gift. I could only find four pop bottles. And nobody wants to hire a seven year old kid. Maybe I can make her something."

Just then she saw another sign in the store window. WE REDEEM COUPONS. "I

know," she said, "I'll make Mother a coupon book."

She went to her room as soon as she got home and got some paper, pencil, scissors and stapler from the desk drawer and began to make a coupon book. When it was finished she wrapped it in plain white paper and tied it with a pretty piece of red yarn. She could hardly wait for Sunday.

That Sunday morning Linda laid her little gift by Mother's plate at the breakfast table. "Happy Mother's Day," she said, placing a kiss on Mother's cheek. "Open it."

Mother pulled the yarn from the carefully wrapped gift and began to read the coupons aloud, with a look of pleasant surprise. "This coupon is good for drying dishes," she said, as she read the first one. "This coupon is good for emptying trash - this coupon is good for making the bed." On she read until all ten coupons were read.

Each one was for some chore or deed of kindness that Linda would do for Mother, cheerfully, upon request. All Mother would have to do, was give Linda a coupon with the chore she wanted done written on it and Linda would cheerfully refund the coupon by doing that chore for Mother.

With tears of happiness in her eyes, Mother gave Linda a big hug and said, "Thank you, Dear, this is the nicest gift you could give because you have given of yourself from the heart."

Linda knew she had made Mother happy. She thought to herself, "From now on I won't grumble every time Mother asks me to do something for her - even after the coupon book is used up."

Phil. 2:14 - *Do all things without murmurings and disputings.*

TUB FUN

FLOATING IN THE BATH-TUB,
  WITH BABY "DIAPER DAN,"
WAS MYRTLE TURTLE, QUACKY DUCK,
  AND PRETTY PETER PAN.

HIS RUBBER BALL AND BOAT,
  WERE ALSO FLOATING THERE,
BUT WAY DOWN ON THE BOTTOM,
  WAS FUZZY TEDDY BEAR.

CLEANLINESS IS NEXT TO GODLINESS

PRETTY LITTLE DARCIE RAE,
  BRUSHED HER TEETH THREE TIMES A DAY.
BRUSHED THEM MORNING, NOON AND NIGHT,
  'TIL THEY WERE SPARKLING CLEAN AND WHITE.

PRETTY LITTLE DARCIE RAE,
  TOOK A TUB BATH EVERY DAY.
SCRUBBED HER ELBOWS, KNEES AND FEET,
  SHE WAS ALWAYS CLEAN AND NEAT.

MY GUARDIAN ANGEL
Ps.91:11-12

I HAVE A GUARDIAN ANGEL.
  HE GOES WITH ME EVERYWHERE,
GOD ABOVE, IN HIS GREAT LOVE,
  ASSIGNED HIM TO MY CARE.

THOUGH I CAN NEVER SEE HIM,
  I DO NOT FEEL ALARM,
FOR YOU SEE, HE WATCHES ME,
  AND KEEPS ME SAFE FROM HARM.

KNOCK, KNOCK

SOMEONE CAME KNOCKING
AT MY HEART'S DOOR.
I HEARD IT AGAIN,
AS I'VE HEARD IT BEFORE.
BUT THIS TIME I OPENED
AND TO MY SURPRISE,
JESUS CAME IN
AND OPENED MY EYES.

Rev. 3:20

41

A CHANGE OF HEART

POOR LITTLE BRIAN
  WAS ALWAYS CRYIN',
'CAUSE RODNEY WOULD
  TEASE AND ACT MEAN.
BUT MOM DIDN'T KNOW
  WHY BRIAN CRIED SO,
FOR THE TEASING
  SHE HAD NOT SEEN.

FINALLY ONE DAY WHEN
  THE BOYS WERE AT PLAY,
AND RODNEY WAS
  UP TO HIS TRICKS,
BRIAN LET OUT A HOLLER,
  THE POOR LITTLE FELLER,
FOR RODNEY HAD
  BROKEN HIS STICKS.

MOM SAW WHAT HE'D DONE -
  SAID, "NOW LISTEN HERE, SON,
YOUR BEHAVIOR DOES
  NOT PLEASE THE LORD.
YOU SHOULD LOVE ONE ANOTHER,
  FOR HE IS YOUR BROTHER,
AS IT IS WRITTEN
  IN HIS WORD."

NOW RODNEY WAS SMART
  AND DEEP IN HIS HEART,
HE KNEW THAT HIS
  MOTHER WAS RIGHT.
HE KNELT BY HIS BED -
  BOWED DOWN HIS HEAD,
AND PRAYED FOR
  FORGIVENESS THAT NIGHT.

THE NEXT DAY AT PLAY,
  IT'S NEEDLESS TO SAY,
THE BOYS PLAYED
  TOGETHER JUST FINE.
FOR RODNEY, YOU SEE,
  ACTED DIFFERENTLY,
HE WAS FILLED
  WITH A LOVE DIVINE.

11 COR. 5:17

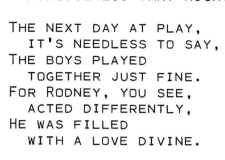

42

GOOD OLD PETE

LISTEN TO THE MUSIC,
    COMING DOWN THE STREET,
AND THE CLIPPITY, CLIPPITY,
    CLOP OF GOOD OLD PETE.
"IT'S THE ICE CREAM WAGON -
    HURRY GET A DIME!"
CHILDREN RUN TO MEET HIM
    AND PETE STOPS JUST IN TIME.

RYAN WANTS A CHOCOLATE -
    MAPLENUT FOR SUE,
STRAWBERRY FOR AMY
    AND ALAINA TOO.
ROYCE PETS OLD PETE
    WHILE HE'S MAKING UP HIS MIND,
THEN FINALLY DECIDES
    TO HAVE THE PURPLE KIND.

PETE STANDS SO PATIENTLY
    WAITING FOR HIS CUE.
AND WHEN THE MUSIC STARTS AGAIN,
    HE KNOWS WHAT TO DO.
HE PULLS THE ICE CREAM WAGON
    SLOWLY DOWN THE STREET,
WHERE CHILDREN RUN AND CALL OUT,
    "HERE COMES GOOD OLD PETE."

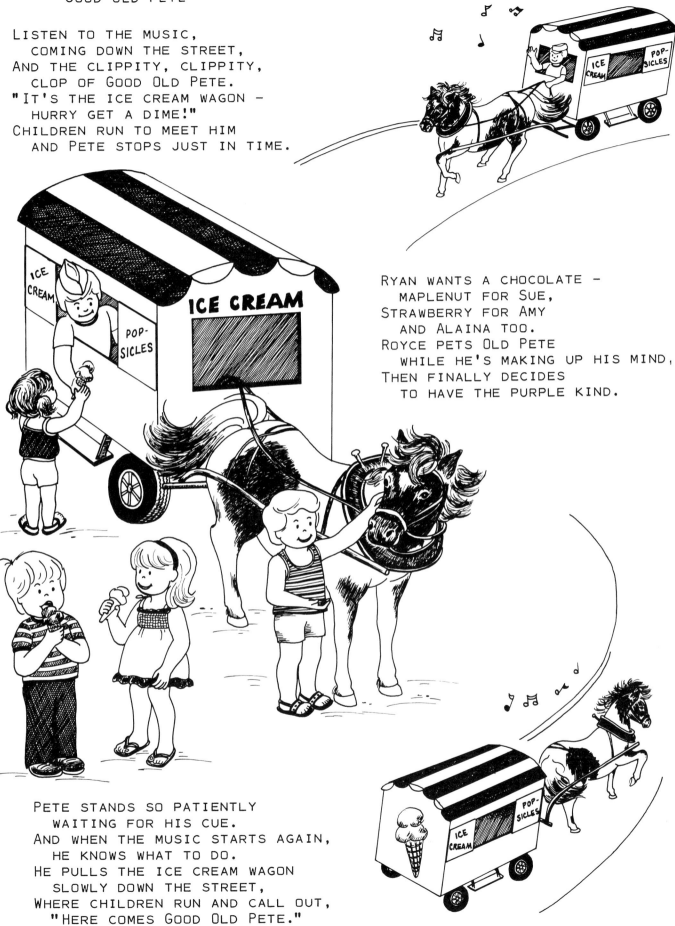

43

HELLO GOD

HELLO, GOD, ARE YOU UP THERE?
  WILL YOU LISTEN TO MY PRAYER?
I HAVE SOMETHING I MUST SAY.
  I ACTED BAD TODAY AT PLAY.

JENNY WANTED MY BEST DOLL.
  I PUSHED HER DOWN AND MADE HER FALL.
THEN SHE CRIED AND WENT BACK HOME,
  AND I HAD TO PLAY ALONE.

NOW I KNOW THAT I WAS WRONG,
  AND I'LL FEEL BAD ALL DAY LONG.
EXCUSE ME, GOD - I'LL WIPE MY EYES,
  THEN I WILL GO APOLOGIZE.

1 JOHN 1:9

TEACH ME, LORD

TEACH ME, LORD,
  YOUR WONDROUS WAYS,
AND I WILL SERVE YOU
  ALL MY DAYS.

I'LL RUN ERRANDS
  FOR GRANDMA MABEL,
AND SWEEP THE WALK
  WHEN SHE'S NOT ABLE.

AND I WILL TEND
  TO BABY JOE,
WHEN MOMMY'S HEAD
  IS HURTING SO.

I'LL TAKE A MEAL
  TO MR. VING,
WHEN HE'S TOO SICK
  TO FIX SOMETHING.

DOING FOR OTHERS
  I HAVE HEARD,
IS SERVING YOU,
  MY PRECIOUS LORD.

MATTHEW 25:40

44

FUN WITH PICTURES

I HAVE A PICTURE ALBUM,
  MY GRANDMA GAVE TO ME.
PICTURE ALBUMS CAN BE FUN.
  I'M SURE YOU WILL AGREE.

I HAVE SO MANY PICTURES,
  OF PLACES I HAVE BEEN.
I HAVE SPENT A LOT OF TIME,
  PASTING THEM ALL IN.

I KEEP IT HIGH UPON THE SHELF,
  AWAY FROM BABY'S HAND,
'CAUSE I DON'T WANT IT RUINED
  SOMEDAY HE'LL UNDERSTAND.

WHEN IT'S COLD AND RAINY OUT,
  AND I MUST STAY INSIDE,
I GET MY PICTURE ALBUM DOWN,
  AND SIT BY FIRESIDE.

Phil. 4:11

THANKSGIVING DAY

HARVEST IS OVER, WORK IS DONE,
  LET US THANK HIM, EVERYONE.
THANKSGIVING DAY AT LAST IS HERE,
  HOW I LOVE THIS TIME OF YEAR.

A TIME FOR FRIENDS AND FAMILY,
  A TIME FOR LOVE AND CHARITY,
A TIME FOR PRAYERS OF GRATITUDE,
  AND GRANDMA'S SPECIAL HOME-COOKED FOOD.

Eph. 5:20

45

There Must Be a God

Margaret A. Lang

Wally Ost

There must be a God, oth-er-wise, Who put the rain-bow in the
There must be a God, oth-er-wise, Who made the sun to set and

skies? Who wrapped the egg in a shell so tight, And Who turns
rise? How does the snow fall from high a - bove, And Who fills

day - light in - to night? There must be a
moth - ers' hearts with love? There must be a

Though I can't see Him, I know He's here. For His mir-a-cles are seen eve-ry-

where!

where!

**Special "Piano and Choral Arrangements"
will be available from the Publisher.**

THERE MUST BE A GOD

THERE MUST BE A GOD — OTHERWISE,
WHO PUT THE RAINBOW IN THE SKIES?
WHO WRAPPED THE EGG IN A SHELL SO TIGHT,
AND WHO TURNS DAYLIGHT INTO NIGHT?

THERE MUST BE A GOD — OTHERWISE,
HOW COULD WORMS CHANGE TO BUTTERFLIES?
HOW COULD THE BALD EAGLE FLY SO HIGH,
AND A BOY BE A MAN BY 'N' BY?

THERE MUST BE A GOD — OTHERWISE,
WHO MADE THE SUN TO SET AND RISE?
HOW DOES THE SNOW FALL FROM HIGH ABOVE,
AND WHO FILLS MOTHERS' HEARTS WITH LOVE?

THERE MUST BE A GOD — OTHERWISE,
WHO MADE TREES EVERY SHAPE AND SIZE?
HOW WOULD THE WILDFLOWERS BLOOM IN SPRING,
AND WHO GAVE BIRDS A SONG TO SING?

YES, THERE'S A GOD, I KNOW IT'S TRUE,
HE CARES FOR ME, AND HE CARES FOR YOU.
THOUGH I CAN'T SEE HIM, I KNOW HE'S HERE,
FOR HIS MIRACLES ARE SEEN EVERYWHERE.

49

LOST AND FOUND

It was a beautiful spring day as the six Wilson children left their farm home early that morning for the little school in the country. It was a three mile walk but they didn't mind when the weather was nice. There was always something different to see along the way while over the prairie, across the creek and through the badlands they went each day.

The prairie animals were beginning to have their young ones out with them. The bunnies and prairie dogs were bashful and always scurried for their hole in the ground when they saw the children coming. The children knew it was smart to keep their distance when they came upon the skunk family.

As they crested the last hill of the way, the school bell began to ring and the children ran hurriedly down the hill toward the school. They didn't want to be late and have to stay in at recess on such a nice day.

The day seemed to never end, for the children were anxious to be out of doors. Finally the teacher announced dismissal and they wasted little time gathering up their books and light spring jackets. "Good - night Miss Owens," they said, hurrying out the door, "see you tomorrow."

Bill and Judy, the two youngest in the family, lagged behind since it had been a long day for them. They were in no real hurry to get home. They

didn't notice the dark clouds building up in the west. Before long it had begun to snow and blow until they could scarcely see where they were going.

Mother was relieved to hear the children come into the porch and went to meet them. "Where's Billy and Judy?" She asked the four older children.

"I don't know," Sarah answered, "I thought they were right behind us."

Mother quickly gathered up some warm coats, bundled herself up and went in search of the two youngsters.

Bill and Judy were getting very cold and tired. It seemed as though they had walked a long way and should be home by now. Judy put her arm around her younger brother and assured him they would be home soon. Silently she asked JESUS to help them find their way.

Just then Judy saw a figure coming through the snow and recognized the call as Mother's. "Thank you, JESUS," she whispered, pulling Bill along. They called back to Mother as they ran to greet her. Mother put the warmer coats and mittens on them and quickly took them home where the others were waiting anxiously.

That night before bed Mother read the story of the good Shepherd, who, having lost one sheep, left the other ninety nine and went in search of the one. When the lost was found there was great rejoicing. (Matt. 18:11-15)

HEAVEN

THERE IS A PLACE MORE LOVELY,
  THAN EVER SEEN BEFORE.
A PLACE WHERE LOVE, PEACE AND JOY
  WILL REIGN FOREVERMORE.

THE LIGHT OF GOD SHINES BRIGHTLY,
  THE STREETS ARE OF PURE GOLD.
FLOWERS ARE BLOOMING EVERYWHERE,
  AND WE SHALL NE'ER GROW OLD.

WALLS ARE MADE OF PRECIOUS STONES,
  AND MANSIONS BUILT SO FAIR.
THE SONGS OF SAINTS AND ANGELS,
  JOYOUSLY FILL THE AIR.

WHERE JESUS IS THE MASTER
  AND ALL HIS NAME PROCLAIM,
SINGING PRAISES TO THE LORD,
  THE LAMB FOR SINNERS SLAIN.

THE GREAT COMMANDMENT

Jesus Said:

"You should love the Lord your God with all your heart and with all your soul and all your mind.

This is the first and great commandment.

And the second is like unto it, you should love your neighbor as yourself."

Matthew 22:37-39

53

LULLABIES

MOTHER SINGS TO BABY,
   THE SONGS SHE SANG TO ME,
WHEN I WAS SMALL LIKE BABY,
   AND SAT UPON HER KNEE.

NOW THAT I'M A BIG GIRL,
   I LIKE TO SING LIKE SHE
THE SONGS SHE SINGS TO BABY,
   TO THE DOLLIE ON MY KNEE.

SLEEPY BABY

MOTHER SINGS SWEET LULLABIES,
BABY SHUTS HIS BIG BLUE EYES.
RESTING ON HER LOVING ARM,
FEELING SAFE FROM ILL OR HARM.
LISTENING TO HIS FAVORITE TUNE,
BABY FALLS ASLEEP REAL SOON.

SWEET MELISSA ROSE

MOMMIE'S LITTLE DARLING,
   WITH A TURNED UP NOSE.
A SMALL GIFT OF LOVE,
   SENT FROM GOD ABOVE,
SWEET MELISSA ROSE.

DADDY'S LITTLE SWEETHEART,
   DRESSED IN SOFT PINK CLOTHES,
SHE COOS LIKE A DOVE,
   SHE'S EASY TO LOVE,
SWEET MELISSA ROSE.

MY TURTLE

I HAD A TURTLE
  HE LIVED IN A SHELL,
I FOUND HIM DOWN
  BY THE WATER WELL.

I THOUGHT IT WAS FUNNY
  WHEN HE SNAPPED AT A BEE,
BUT IT WASN'T FUNNY
  WHEN HE SNAPPED AT ME.

HE PINCHED MY FINGER
  AND HE MADE ME CRY,
IT HURT ME SO
  I THOUGHT I WOULD DIE.

I SCREAMED AND I SCREAMED
  'TIL HE FINALLY LET GO.
I RAN TO MOTHER
  AS MY TEARS DID FLOW.

NOW I LEARNED A LESSON
  AS THE SAYING GOES,
"KEEP YOUR FINGERS AWAY
  FROM THE TURTLE'S NOSE."

NAUGHTY HEIDI

JOSEPHINE, JOSEPHINE,
WHY DO YOU CRY?
I CRY BECAUSE HEIDI
ATE ALL THE PIE.

HEIDI, HEIDI,
ME OH MY!
WHY DID YOU
EAT ALL THE PIE?

THE RAINBOW
*GEN. 9:12-13

I LOOKED ACROSS THE CLOUDY SKY,
AND THERE A RAINBOW DID I SPY.

THEN I REMEMBERED, LONG AGO,
GOD DID SET THE FIRST RAINBOW,*

AS A PROMISE FROM OUR LORD,
HE WILL ALWAYS KEEP HIS WORD.

NO MORE WILL RAIN DESTROY THE EARTH,
BUT ONLY GIVE IT A NEW BIRTH.

BRINGING FLOWERS AND THE GRAIN,
TO ONCE A DRY AND BARREN PLAIN.

NOW WHEN A RAINBOW SPANS THE BLUE,
I'M REMINDED - GOD'S WORD IS TRUE.

IN THE BEGINNING GOD CREATED -
GENESIS: 1

I KNOW GOD MADE THE FLOWERS.
 HE MADE THE BIG OAK TREE.
HE MADE THE BIRDS AND ANIMALS,
 AND HE MADE YOU - AND ME.

HE CLOTHES THE TREES AND FLOWERS,
 THE BIRDS AND ANIMALS HE FEEDS.
HE WATCHES OVER LITTLE CHILDREN,
 AND SUPPLIES THEIR EVERY NEEDS.

57

GOD'S WORKERS

TODAY I WATCHED A SQUIRREL,
    AS HE WORKED SO CHEERFULLY,
STORING HIS FOOD FOR WINTER,
    IN HIS HOME UP IN THE TREE.

I WATCHED THE BUSY ANTS,
    AS THEY HURRIED TO AND FRO,
GATHERING TINY MORSELS,
    TO HELP THEIR SMALL ONES GROW.

FROM BLOSSOM TO BLOSSOM,
    BUZZED THE LITTLE HONEY BEE,
MAKING HONEY FOR HIMSELF,
    AND SOME FOR YOU AND ME.

THIS IS THE WAY GOD PLANNED IT,
    THAT ALL SHOULD EARN THEIR KEEP.
"IF ANY WOULD NOT WORK,
    (THEN) NEITHER SHOULD HE EAT."

11 THESS. 3:10

WATCHING THE GARDEN GROW

IT WAS A WARM DAY,
    ON THE TENTH OF MAY,
WHEN WE PLANTED THE GARDEN SPOT.
    WE PLANTED VEGETABLES,
OF MOST EVERY KIND,
    IN THE FAR CORNER OF THE LOT.
WE HOED, WE WATERED,
    AND PULLED UP THE WEEDS,
AND TRUSTED IN GOD FOR THE REST.
    THEN WHEN IT WAS TIME,
TO GATHER THEM IN,
    WE THANKED GOD AND ATE THEM WITH ZEST.

(1 COR. 3:6-9)

FIRST DAY OF SCHOOL

IT WAS THE FIRST DAY OF SCHOOL,
  AND BILLY COULD HARDLY WAIT.
HE GOT UP EARLY THAT MORNING,
  'CAUSE HE DIDN'T WANT TO BE LATE.

HE ATE A GOOD HOT BREAKFAST,
  AND BRUSHED HIS TEETH SO CLEAN.
HE COMBED HIS HAIR, AND LOOKED TO BE,
  THE NEATEST BOY YOU'VE EVER SEEN.

HE WAVED GOOD-BYE TO HIS MOTHER,
  AND HURRIED ON DOWN THE STREET.
BUT WHEN HE CAME FROM SCHOOL THAT NIGHT,
  YOUNG BILLY BOY WASN'T SO NEAT.

LOST TOOTH

DADDY PULLED MY TOOTH FOR ME.
IT WASN'T TOO MUCH FUN.
BUT IN ANOTHER WEEK OR SO,
I'LL HAVE A BRAND NEW ONE.

WHAT IS LOVE?---

I Cor. 13:4-8

Love is gentle

Love is kind

Love is tender

Love is blind

Love is helping

Love is caring

Love is giving

Love is sharing

JESUS SAID: "BY THIS SHALL ALL MEN KNOW THAT YOU ARE MY
DISCIPLES, IF YOU HAVE LOVE ONE TO ANOTHER." JOHN 13:35

A BIRD IN THE HAND

Quietly David crept up to the little bird sitting on the currant bush in the back yard. He had been watching the birds flutter about most of the afternoon. Remembering that he had learned in church how GOD even cares for the little sparrows, David thought how nice it would be if he had a bird of his very own to care for.

Perhaps if he were very quick and very careful he could catch one. He was about to reach for the bird when suddenly it flew to another bush near-by. It seemed as though every time he nearly had a bird in his hands, it would quickly fly away.

He had tried every way he knew to catch a bird. His little dog Dixie knew what David was trying to do and she did her best to help too. Finally in desperation, he went to the house to see if Mother would come help him.

"Mom," he said, as he came into the kitchen, "I've tried and tried to catch a bird and they always fly away. Will you help me?"

Now Mother was busy making cookies and couldn't leave

the kitchen right then. "Son," she said, "Have you asked GOD for a bird? Why don't you pray about it?"

"Wow!" he exclaimed, "that's a good idea. I never thought of that." David knew that if you love JESUS with all your heart and believe on Him, whatsoever you ask GOD in JESUS' name, it shall be done. (John 14:13-14) He hurried to his room to have a talk with GOD and in a few minutes he was back outside trying again to catch a bird, confident that GOD would help him.

He was still trying very hard when Mother called him to the phone. It was Mrs. Abel from across the street. "David," she said, "I was wondering if you would like to have my parakeet? I am going to live with my daughter and won't be able to take it with me. You may have the cage too if you want it."

David could scarcely believe his ears. "You bet!" he said and hung up the phone. He called back to Mother as he ran out the door, "GOD answered my prayer. I have a bird and a cage."

"Suffer (allow) little children and forbid them not to come unto me, for of such is the kingdom of heaven." Matthew 19:14

ME, MYSELF AND I

I WAS LONESOME AND ALONE.
  NOT A FRIEND TO CALL MY OWN.
ALL I THOUGHT ABOUT WAS ME,
  OTHER'S NEEDS I DID NOT SEE.

NOT THEIR WORRIES OR THEIR FEARS,
  NOT THEIR PROBLEMS NOR THEIR CARES,
ONLY ME, MYSELF, AND I,
  CONCERNED ME AS THE DAYS WENT BY.

MORE AND MORE I WAS ALONE.
  MORE AND MORE I STAYED AT HOME.
OTHER KIDS AVOIDED ME,
  I WAS UNHAPPY AS COULD BE.

THEN MY MOTHER SAID TO ME,
  "LISTEN, CHILD, CAN'T YOU SEE,
IF YOU WANT FRIENDS, YOU SHOULD KNOW,
  TO OTHERS, FRIENDSHIP YOU MUST SHOW.

TRY TO LIVE THE GOLDEN RULE,
  BEING KIND AND NEVER CRUEL.
LOVE YOUR NEIGHBOR AS YOURSELF,
  PUT YOUR FEELINGS ON THE SHELF."

SINCE I'VE LIVED THE GOLDEN RULE,
  I HAVE LOTS OF FRIENDS AT SCHOOL.
TO PUT OTHERS FIRST, I TRY,
  FORGETTING ME, MYSELF AND I.

NOW I'M HAPPY AS CAN BE,
  SINCE I PUT OTHERS BEFORE ME.

Matt. 7:12

SLEDDING

A VERY FINE LAD
  NAMED CHRISTOPHER WILL,
CALLED TO HIS FRIEND,
  MISS JENNIFER JILL,
TO MEET HIM AT
  THE TOP OF THE HILL,
SO HE COULD DEMONSTRATE
  HIS SLEDDING SKILL.

HE RODE HIS SLED
  DOWN THE BIG LONG HILL,
AND WAS DOING
  VERY WELL UNTIL
THE SLED HIT A BUMP
  AND HE TOOK A SPILL.
HE JUMPED RIGHT UP
  OR HE'D BE THERE STILL.

THE SNOW ON HIS FACE
  GAVE HIM QUITE A CHILL.
OF THE SLEDDING FUN
  HE'D HAD HIS FILL.
SO HE PULLED HIS SLED
  BACK UP THE HILL,
AND OFFERED A RIDE
  TO JENNIFER JILL.

SHE GOT ON THE SLED
  OF HER OWN FREE WILL,
AND STARTED ON DOWN
  THE BIG LONG HILL.
SHE WENT SO FAST -
  IT WAS QUITE A THRILL,
AND KEPT ON GOING
  CLEAR TO CUSTERVILLE.

SHE CAME TO A STOP
  BY THE OLD WINDMILL,
AND IT WASN'T
  VERY LONG UNTIL,
SHE WAS BACK ON TOP
  OF THE BIG LONG HILL,
BEAMING AND SMILING
  AT CHRISTOPHER WILL.

Now Christopher Will
   was feeling ill
'Cause he'd been bested
   by Jennifer Jill.
So he thought he'd try
   again his skill,
And ride once more
   down the big long hill.

He said, "Jump on,
   Miss Jennifer Jill,
I'll show you how
   to conquer this hill."
To prove he didn't
   hold any ill-will,
Together they rode
   toward the old windmill.

They only got half-
   way down the hill,
When with all that weight,
   the sled stopped still,
But Jennifer Jill
   and Christopher Will,
Tumbled and rolled
   to the foot of the hill.

They brushed off the snow
   'fore they got a chill,
And laughed at themselves
   'cause they looked so sill.
And for all I know
   they're laughing still,
By the old windmill
   at the foot of the hill,
(In Custerville).

GOOD INTENTIONS

ONE WARM DAY, AFTER THE RAIN,
  ELIZABETH WANTED TO PLAY.
SHE STARTED FOR THE OUT-OF-DOORS,
  AND MOTHER PROCEEDED TO SAY,

"DON'T GET MUD ON YOUR CLOTHES, DEAR,
  TRY TO KEEP THEM NICE AND CLEAN.
FOR WE ARE GOING TO HARDIN,
  TO VISIT YOUR AUNT MARLENE."

ELIZABETH WAS A GOOD GIRL,
  AND SHE WOULDN'T DISOBEY.
SHE LISTENED VERY CAREFULLY,
  TO WHAT MOTHER HAD TO SAY.

SO WHEN SHE WENT OUTSIDE TO PLAY,
  JUST WHAT DO YOU SUPPOSE?
TO KEEP FROM GETTING THEM MUDDY,
  SHE TOOK OFF ALL HER CLOTHES.

COMPANY

COMPANY CAME TO OUR HOUSE.
"THERE'S ALWAYS ROOM FOR ONE MORE."
BUT WHEN IT WAS TIME TO GO TO BED,
I HAD TO SLEEP ON THE FLOOR.

68

GOOD NIGHT, JESUS

GOOD NIGHT, JESUS,
  AND THANKS AGAIN,
FOR FORGIVING ME
  OF ALL MY SIN.

FOR BEING WITH ME
  THROUGH THE DAY,
AND WATCHING O'ER ME
  AT SCHOOL AND PLAY.

THANKS FOR BEING
  MY SPECIAL FRIEND.
I KNOW, ON YOU,
  I CAN DEPEND.

AND IN THE MORN,
  WHEN I AWAKE,
HELP ME BE GOOD,
  FOR JESUS' SAKE.

AMEN

MORE LIKE JESUS

PLEASE, JESUS, HELP ME TO BE
  MORE LIKE YOU AND LESS LIKE ME.
WHEN I'M MAD AND WEAR A FROWN,
  HELP ME TO TURN IT UPSIDE DOWN.

WHEN I'M SELFISH WITH MY TOYS,
  HELP ME TO SHARE WITH OTHER BOYS.
IF I ACT MEAN AND TEASE OR POUT,
  HELP ME TO TURN IT ALL ABOUT.

I WANT TO BE MUCH MORE LIKE YOU
  AND DO THE THINGS YOU WANT ME TO.
SO IF YOU'LL FILL MY HEART WITH JOY,
  THEN I WILL BE A NICER BOY.

Phil. 4:13

THE POOR WIDOW

A very long time ago in the city of Jerusalem JESUS was at the temple teaching in parables to all who would listen. A parable is a short story used to tell a truth or teach a moral lesson.

While he was there, JESUS sat over against the treasury and watched how the people put money into the treasury of the temple as an offering to GOD. Many that were rich and dressed in fine clothes put in a lot of money. Then there came a certain poor widow lady dressed very poorly, and she cast in two little mites, which make a farthing, and that's not very much money.

JESUS called the diciples over to him and said, "Verily I say unto you, that this poor widow has put more in than all they which cast into the treasury. For they all cast in of their abundance." Meaning they were rich and could have put in a lot more than they did. "But she, even though she is poor, cast in all that she had, even all her living."

JESUS doesn't pay any attention to whether or not we are dressed in beautiful expensive clothes he looks into the heart.

Mark 12:41-44

MERRY MARY

MARY ALWAYS WORE A SMILE,
SHE WAS SO SWEET AND CHEERY.
SHE'D SKIP AND SING FOR A COUNTRY MILE,
THAT'S WHY THEY CALLED HER MERRY.

Prov. 17:22

"OOPS"

I RAN TO GET MY COAT ON,
SO I COULD GO UPTOWN.
I QUICKLY PUT MY ARMS IN,
BUT I HAD IT UP-SIDE-DOWN.

THOU SHALT NOT LIE

WHEN TROUBLE SEEMS TO FIND YOU
    AND YOU START TO TELL A LIE,
YOU'D BETTER THINK IT OVER
    THE BIBLE TELLS YOU WHY.

"LYING LIPS ARE AN ABOMINATION
TO THE LORD; BUT THEY THAT DEAL
TRULY ARE HIS DELIGHT." *Pr.12:22*

SO TELL THE TRUTH — NO MATTER WHAT
    FOR THAT'S THE THING TO DO.
AND WHEN YOU START TO TELL A LIE,
    REMEMBER TO BE TRUE.

"A FALSE WITNESS SHALL NOT BE
UNPUNISHED — HE THAT SPEAKETH
LIES SHALL PERISH." *Proverbs 19:9*

IF I HAD WINGS

If GOD HAD GIVEN ME SOME WINGS,
  I'D FLY UP TO THE SKIES,
I'D FLY ABOVE THE TREE-TOPS HIGH,
  AND CATCH SOME BUTTERFLIES.

I'D FLY AWAY TO GRANDMA'S HOUSE.
  WE'D FEAST ON HONEY-COMB.
AND BEFORE THE NIGHT WOULD COME,
  I'D FLY AWAY BACK HOME.

WHEN I WOULD GO TO BED AT NIGHT,
  I'D FOLD MY WINGS UP NICE,
AND PUT THEM IN THE CEDAR CHEST,
  TO KEEP THEM FROM THE MICE.

A PRAYER FOR MOTHER

ONCE MOTHER HAD A HEADACHE,
AND SHE FELL ASLEEP IN THE CHAIR.
I PRAYED FOR HER, AND WHEN SHE AWOKE,
HER HEADACHE WASN'T THERE.

Pray one for another that you may be healed. **James 5:16**

72

CAMPING OUT

FRIEND LYLE AND I WENT CAMPING,
  IN THE MIDDLE OF MY BACK YARD,
PITCHING THE TENT
  WAS QUITE AN EVENT,
FOR WE HAD TO WORK VERY HARD.

WHEN FINALLY THE TENT WAS STANDING,
  AND THE SUN WAS SINKING LOW,
WE JUMPED IN OUR BEDS
  AND COVERED OUR HEADS,
PRETENDING WE WERE IN MEXICO.

WE TALKED ABOUT ARMADILLOS,
  AND ABOUT THE WILD BOARS.
THEN AFTER A WHILE
  MY GOOD FRIEND LYLE,
IMAGINED HE HEARD LION ROARS.

OUR STORIES WERE GETTING WILDER,
  AND THE FUN HAD JUST BEGUN,
WHEN A NOISE IN THE NIGHT
  GAVE US QUITE A FRIGHT,
AND WE WENT TO THE HOUSE ON THE RUN.

Phil. 4:8

73

A LESSON LEARNED

"I'll fix her!" six year old Maggie said aloud. She was very angry with her older sister Nell. Maggie knew better than to start a real fight with Nell, for Nell was bigger and stronger than she.

The two little girls had been sent out to the prairie to herd the sheep that morning. Riding double on their old horse Tony, Nell had kicked the horse in the flank to make him run and Maggie fell off the back. Nell made her walk the rest of the way.

When they arrived at the sheep wagon Maggie sat on the ground and picked the thistles and hay-needles out of her stocking tops. She thought, "I know how I can get even with Nell!"

Later that day Nell left Maggie at the wagon to watch the flock nearby while she rode old Tony out on the prairie to look for lost or strayed sheep. Now, as Maggie sat poking stickery hay-needles into Nell's coat, she thought to herself, "just wait 'til she sees all these hay-needles in her coat."

She held the coat up and looked at all the stickery hay-needles with smug satisfaction. "There!" she said, "that'll fix her!" Just then a trickle of blood came oozing from Maggie's nose. "Oh, no!" she said. She'd had nose bleeds before and she knew how hard it was to get them stopped. Now she was alone. She didn't know what to do. She held her hanky to her face but soon it was soaked. The blood kept right on running.

Before long Nell came over

the top of the hill leading Tony and carrying a lamb in her arms. When she saw Maggie with blood on her face and down her front, she told her to go into the wagon and lay quietly while she rode to get Mother.

Old Tony, who normally didn't like to run, seemed to sense the urgency of the return trip home, for he wasted no time getting there. Soon Mother and Nell returned to the sheep wagon. Mother stuffed cotton in Maggie's nose and placed a cool wet cloth on the back of her neck and over her face until the bleeding was stopped.

Maggie was grateful to Nell for going so quickly to get Mother. Now she was sorry for the way she felt toward Nell earlier that day. She wished she hadn't filled Nell's coat with stickery hay-needles.

That evening when the sheep were back at the ranch safely in their pens for the night, Maggie sat on the porch steps with Nell. "Thank you, Nell, for going after Mother. I'm sorry I filled your coat with those old hay-needles. I'll pull them out again."

"That's okay, Maggie," Nell said, "I'm sorry I wasn't very nice to you this morning either. I'll help you pull them out."

Together the girls sat pulling the hay-needles out of the coat. Each one realizing how much they really loved one another and making a silent promise to themselves, and to GOD, to be better to each other from then on.

JESUS said, "This is my commandment, that ye love one another, as I have loved you." John 15:12.

GOD'S HOUSE

I WAS GLAD WHEN THEY SAID UNTO ME,
  "LET'S GO INTO THE HOUSE OF THE LORD.
FOR I WANT TO BE CLOSER TO GOD,
  AND LEARN MORE OF HIS HOLY WORD.
                    PS. 122:1
AND I LOVE TO HEAR THE OLD STORY,
  HOW GOD SENT HIS BELOVED SON,
THAT I MIGHT BE WHOLLY FORGIVEN,
  AND BE COUNTED AS A "CHOSEN ONE."
                    JOHN 3:16
FOR IT IS BY FAITH IN CHRIST JESUS,
  THAT WE ARE ALL CHILDREN OF GOD,
SO I'LL DO MY BEST TO PLEASE HIM,
  AS THROUGH THIS LIFE ON EARTH I TROD.
                    GAL. 3:26

I LOVE JESUS

I LOVE JESUS, YES I DO,
  AND I KNOW HE LOVES ME TOO.
JESUS SAVIOUR, JESUS FRIEND,
  I WILL LOVE HIM 'TIL THE END.

PEACEFUL NIGHT'S REST

LAST NIGHT WHEN I WENT TO BED,
  I COULD NOT GO TO SLEEP.
I TRIED TO CLOSE MY EYES REAL TIGHT,
  AND COUNT A HUNDRED SHEEP.

BUT THAT DIDN'T SEEM TO WORK,
  SO I BEGAN TO PRAY,
AND ALMOST 'FORE I KNEW IT,
  LAST-NIGHT BECAME TODAY.

                    Psalm 4:8

MY LAMB, ABRAHAM

I HAVE A LITTLE FUZZY LAMB,
   DRESSED IN A WHITE WOOL SUIT.
I LOVE THAT LITTLE LAMB OF MINE.
   HE IS SO SOFT AND CUTE.

HE FOLLOWS ME WHERE'ER HE CAN.
   BUT WHEN I GO TO BED,
SINCE HE CANNOT COME INSIDE,
   HE SLEEPS OUT IN THE SHED.

HE LOVES TO RUN AND JUMP AND PLAY,
   LIKE ANY OTHER LAMB,
AND BECAUSE HE IS SO FAITHFUL,
   I NAMED HIM ABRAHAM.

WHEN I FEED HIM FROM A BOTTLE,
   FRESH MILK SO WARM AND SWEET,
HIS TAIL WIGGLES HIM SO FAST,
   IT KNOCKS HIM OFF HIS FEET.

Gal. 3:9

PLUMS FOR SALE

THE WILD PLUMS LAID ON THE GROUND.
THEY HAD FALLEN ALL AROUND.
I PICKED UP ALL THAT I HAD FOUND,
AND SOLD THEM FOR A NICKEL A POUND.

A NEW THUMB NAIL

I SMASHED MY THUMB IN THE CAR DOOR.
IT TURNED ALL BLACK AND BLUE.
BEFORE MANY DAYS, MY THUMB NAIL CAME OFF,
AND A PRETTY NEW THUMB NAIL GREW.

THE FIRST SNOWFALL OF WINTER

I WOKE UP THIS MORNING
  TO QUITE A SURPRISE,
FOR SNOWFLAKES WERE FALLING
  FROM THE GREY SKIES.
THEY FELL ON THE ROOF TOPS
  AND TREES ALL AROUND.
THE BEAUTIFUL SNOW
  HAD COVERED THE GROUND.

AFTER BUILDING A SNOWMAN
  FIT FOR A KING,
MY FINGERS AND TOES
  ALL BEGAN TO STING.
MY MITTENS WERE WET
  AND MY CHEEKS WERE ROSY.
I WENT IN TO WARM
  BY THE FIRE SO COZY.

I HURRIED THROUGH BREAKFAST
  AS FAST AS I COULD.
AND PUTTING ON ALL
  THE WARM CLOTHES THAT I SHOULD,
I WENT OUT TO PLAY
  IN THE FRESH FALLEN SNOW,
BLAZING NEW TRAILS
  WHEREVER I'D GO.

I LOOKED AT THE CLOCK —
  IT REGISTERED NOON.
I DIDN'T DREAM
  IT WAS LUNCH TIME SO SOON.
THE TIME WENT SO FAST —
  I KNOW NOT WHERE,
BUT I'M HUNGRY ENOUGH
  TO EAT A BEAR.

"GOOD MORNING"

THIS MORNING AS I ROSE FROM BED,
  I LOOKED OUT TO THE SKY,
THE MORNING SUN WAS SHINING,
  AND BIRDS WERE FLYING BY.

I COULD SMELL THE BACON FRYING,
  AS MOTHER SANG HAPPILY.
AND I HURRIED IN TO HUG HER,
  FOR ALL SHE DOES FOR ME.

THEN I SAT AT THE TABLE,
  AND BOWED MY HEAD TO PRAY.
"THANK YOU FOR THIS FOOD, DEAR LORD,
  AND FOR ANOTHER DAY."

I Thes. 5:18

79

DEAR JESUS, I PRAY -

GIVE ME A HEART IN TUNE WITH THEE, LORD.
HELP ME TO UNDERSTAND THY WORD.

GIVE ME TWO EYES THY GLORIES TO SEE.
MAKE A MORE THANKFUL PERSON OF ME.

GIVE ME TWO EARS THAT I MIGHT HEAR,
THE SONGS OF ANGELS AS THEY PASS NEAR.

GIVE ME TWO LEGS THY PATHS TO WALK,
A MOUTH THAT'S QUICK, OF THY LOVE, TO TALK.

GIVE ME TWO LIPS THY PRAISES TO SING,
AS ALL OF ME, TO THEE, I BRING.

GIVE ME A SPIRIT OF LOVE I PRAY,
THAT I MIGHT HELP OTHERS TO FIND THY WAY.

AMEN

THE SUCKER-TREE

I WALKED INTO THE RESTAURANT,
  WITH GRANDPA ONE SUMMER DAY,
AND WHAT SHOULD I SEE,
  BUT A BIG SUCKER-TREE,
WITH BIG SUCKERS ALL ON DISPLAY.

THERE WERE SUCKERS EVERY COLOR,
  EVERY SHAPE AND EVERY SIZE.
I NEVER DID SEE,
  SUCH A BIG SUCKER TREE.
I COULD SCARCELY BELIEVE MY EYES.

GRANDPA SAID IF I ATE MY LUNCH,
  HE WOULD BUY ONE FOR ME AND SIS,
AND YOU BET I DID,
  LIKE A GOOD LITTLE KID,
AND GAVE GRANDPA A GREAT BIG KISS.

81

HAPPY DAYS

Quincee waved goodby to her mother and little sister, Darcie, as the motor home pulled away from the curb. What fun she was going to have! Five whole days with Grandma and Grandpa.

Grandma and Grandpa lived in a motor home and traveled all over the United States because of their work. Quincee didn't get to see them very often so when Grandma asked Mother if Quincee could go with them on a short trip into Wyoming, Quincee was hoping Mother would say yes. She had never been away from home for such a long time and had never slept in a motor home.

When they drove into the first little town in Wyoming, Grandpa suggested that Grandma and Quincee spend some time in the city park while he called on the businesses in town. That sounded good to Quincee for there wasn't any park in her home town.

She went down the slide and rode the merry-go-'round. Then she tried the swing. Grandma pushed her higher and higher as she tried to reach the clouds with her toes. She was having so much fun, but every now and then she thought of Darcie and wished she could be here too, although she knew that Darcie was much too little to leave Mother for so long a time.

Grandma and Quincee visited the park in every town they went while Grandpa worked. One night after work Grandpa took them out for dinner. As Quincee was eating, what should she see, but the biggest sucker tree she ever saw in her whole life! Grandpa promised her, if she would eat all her dinner, he would get one for her and one to take home for Darcie. Of course she didn't need much coaxing and soon she had two BIG suckers in her hand.

Quincee must have fallen asleep while the motor home was homeward bound the next day. When she opened her eyes they had just arrived in another little town. "Something must be going on," she said, "look at all the people!"

"Yes," Grandpa said, "I saw a fair when we drove into town."

"Let's hurry over there, Quincee, and see what's going on," said Grandma, as she helped the little girl put on her shoes.

Quincee had never been at a fair, so she could hardly wait to get there. She took Grandma's hand and together they ran down the sidewalk toward the crowd of people. She could hear the music and smell the popcorn as they got closer to the fairgrounds.

Grandma bought some tickets and soon Quincee was on the merry-go-'round. It seemed as though the music was playing just for her. She rode the airplanes, whirly tubs, little farris wheel and roller coaster too. Grandma rode with her on some of them. When she had been on them all and some of them twice, they stopped at the concession stand and bought some popcorn, cotton candy and orange drink.

"Wait 'til I tell Mother and Darcie about the fair," said Quincee when they were leaving. "I wish Darcie could have been here too. Let's get something to take home for her. I have some money." Together they went shopping.

It didn't take Quincee long to find just the thing Darcie would like. She knew how Darcie loved baby dolls and this little Raggedy Ann doll would make her very happy.

Quincee was happy too, for she was learning to live by the Golden Rule. And what is the Golden Rule? Why, JESUS said, we should do unto others what we'd want them to do unto us (Matt. 7:12).

THE COUNTY FAIR

WHEN I WENT TO THE COUNTY FAIR,
I HEARD MUSIC IN THE AIR.
THERE WERE PEOPLE EVERYWHERE,
AT THE COUNTY FAIR.

I WENT IN AND PAID THE FARE,
LOOKED AROUND AND FOUND A CHAIR,
WATCHED THE TRAINER WITH HIS BEAR,
AT THE COUNTY FAIR.

THEN THERE CAME, FROM WHERESOE'ER,
A PRETTY MAIDEN WITH LONG HAIR,
RIDING ON A SILVER MARE,
AT THE COUNTY FAIR.

NEXT A CLOWN IN UNDERWEAR,
  SAT DOWN ON A PRICKLY-PEAR,
DID A DANCE IN SOLITAIRE,
  AT THE COUNTY FAIR.

A YOUNG MAN FROM DELAWARE,
  LOOKING VERY DEBONAIR,
SHOT FROM A CANNON ON A DARE,
  AT THE COUNTY FAIR.

I ATE COTTON-CANDY THERE,
  CARAMELED APPLE AND A PEAR,
POPCORN, HOT DOG, AND WHATE'ER,
  AT THE COUNTY FAIR.

THOUGH I FELT LIKE A MILLIONAIRE,
  I WAS VERY BROKE HOWE'ER.
I'D SPENT IT ALL UNAWARE,
  AT THE COUNTY FAIR.

BROOM-STICK COWBOY

DADDY'S LITTLE COWBOY,
  RIDING MOMMA'S BROOM,
ROUNDING UP THE CATTLE,
  IN THE LIVING ROOM.

'ROUND AND 'ROUND THE CHAIR,
  AND O'ER THE FOOT-STOOL,
GATHERING IN THE HORSES,
  AND THE OLD GREY MULE.

WHEN HE GOT TIRED,
  HE TOOK OFF HIS HAT,
AND LAID ON THE FLOOR,
  BY THE OLD TOM CAT.

THEN HE PUT HIS HAND,
  ON TOM'S SOFT WHITE FUR,
AND FELL FAST ASLEEP,
  LISTENING TO HIM PURR.

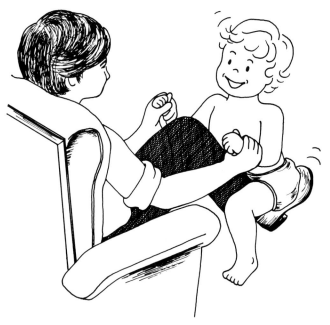

HORSY RIDE

UP, DOWN, UP, DOWN,
  RIDING THE HORSY IS FUN.
WHEN THE HORSY IS TIRED,
  I GET ON THE OTHER ONE.

IF THE HORSY WERE STRONGER,
  AND DIDN'T GET TIRED SO SOON,
I'D JUST KEEP RIGHT ON RIDING,
  'TIL MORNING TURNED INTO NOON.

86

WHICH WAY TO HEAVEN?

WHICH IS THE WAY TO HEAVEN?
  I'D REALLY LIKE TO KNOW.
'CAUSE WHEN MY LIFE ON EARTH IS DONE,
  THAT'S WHERE I WANT TO GO.

SOME SAY THIS WAY — SOME SAY THAT.
  IT IS SO CONFUSING.
THERE MUST BE ONLY ONE TRUE WAY.
  WHICH WAY SHOULD I BE CHOOSING?

JESUS SAID, "I AM THE WAY.
  THERE IS NO OTHER WAY."
IF WE LIVE FOR HIM ON EARTH,
  WE'LL MEET IN HEAVEN SOME DAY.

JOHN 14:6

GOD'S PLAN FOR OUR SALVATION

For all have sinned (Rom. 3:23) and the wages of sin is death, but the gift of GOD is eternal life through JESUS CHRIST our LORD.

(Rom. 6:23)

For GOD so loved the world that He gave His only begotton Son, that whosoever believes in Him should not perish but have everlasting life.

(John 3:16)

While we were yet sinners Christ died for us. (Rom. 5:8) We are redeemed by His blood and forgiven of sin.

(Eph. 1:7)

88

Christ being raised from the dead dies no more. (Rom. 6:9-12) If you confess with your mouth the LORD JESUS and believe in your heart that GOD raised Him from the dead, you will be saved from your sins. **(Rom. 10:9-10)**

Repent, and be baptized every one of you in the name of JESUS CHRIST for the remission of sins, and you shall receive the gift of the Holy Ghost. **(Acts 2:38)**

He that believes and is baptized will be saved, but he that does not believe will be damned. **(Mark 16:16)**

MY BROTHER'S KEEPER

WHILE MOTHER'S WORKING VERY HARD,
  I WATCH BROTHER IN THE YARD.
I KEEP HIM FROM THE THORNY ROSE,
  AND TRY TO WIPE HIS RUNNY NOSE.

I PULL HIM IN MY WAGON RED,
  AND FIX HIM UP WITH JELLY-BREAD.
THEN I ROCK HIM ON MY LAP,
  WHEN HE'S READY FOR HIS NAP.

GUY

THERE WAS A YOUNG MAN NAMED GUY.
HE WANTED TO LEARN HOW TO FLY.
SO HE MADE SOME WINGS
OUT OF CARDBOARD AND STRINGS -
BUT DAD STOPPED HIM BEFORE HE COULD TRY.

CHILDREN OBEY YOUR PARENTS IN ALL THINGS,
FOR THIS IS WELL PLEASING UNTO THE LORD.

COL. 3:20

A SECRET TO TELL

I KNOW A SECRET I MUST TELL,
HOW JESUS MADE THE SICK MAN WELL,
MADE THE BLIND TO SEE AND THE LAME TO WALK,
THE DEAF TO HEAR AND THE DUMB TO TALK.

HE CHANGED THE WATER INTO WINE,
CAST THE DEMONS INTO SWINE.
HE RAISED UP LAZARUS FROM THE DEAD,
AND CLEANSED THE LEPER FROM TOES TO HEAD.

OF COURSE THERE'S MANY MORE TO TELL,
BUT I DON'T KNOW THEM ALL TOO WELL,
SO WHILE I'M GROWING TO BE A MAN,
I'LL READ MY BIBLE AND LEARN ALL I CAN.
2 Tim. 2:15

Acts 10:38

91

SPRING

LONG COLD NIGHTS OF WINTER PAST,
   WARM SUNNY DAYS ARE HERE AT LAST.
SNOW HAS MELTED - GRASS IS GREEN.
   BIRDS HAVE ALL BEGUN TO SING.

BABY BUNNIES HERE AND THERE,
   BUTTERFLIES ARE IN THE AIR,
BUDS ON BUSHES - LEAVES ON TREES.
   SMELL THE BLOSSOMS IN THE BREEZE.

TULIPS PUSHING THROUGH THE GROUND,
   FLOWERS BLOOMING ALL AROUND,
BOYS WITH THEIR KITES FLYING HIGH,
   GIRLS PLAY 'JUMPING-ROPE' NEARBY.

MOTHER'S DIGGING IN THE YARD.
   FATHER'S WORKING VERY HARD.
THE WHOLE WORLD COMES ALIVE,
   WHEN AT LAST SPRING DOES ARRIVE.

92

THANK YOU GOD

IF I WERE A ROBIN,
   I'D SIT UP IN MY TREE,
AND I'D SING MY VERY SWEETEST SONG,
   TO THANK GOD FOR MAKING ME.

IF I WERE A FUZZY WORM,
   I'D BE BUSY AS CAN BE,
AND I'D WIGGLE THE BEST I KNOW HOW,
   TO THANK GOD FOR MAKING ME.

IF I WERE A KITTY,
   I'D BE HAPPY ALL DAY, YOU SEE.
I'D PURR THE LOUDEST YOU EVER HEARD,
   TO THANK GOD FOR MAKING ME.

BUT SINCE I'M JUST A LITTLE CHILD,
   AND CAN'T SING LIKE ROBINS SING,
THEN I'LL BE THE BEST THAT I KNOW HOW,
   TO THANK GOD FOR EVERYTHING.

MARY PONESSA

KIT FOR CAT

As the loaded car pulled away from the little white house that had been Larry's home for all of his seven years, he waved good-by to Janet. She was holding his black and white cat in her arms, lovingly stroking his soft furry body.

Larry flicked the tear off his cheek with his finger. He didn't like having to leave Tuffy behind, but he knew it would be a long hot trip for the cat. The family had agreed that it was best to leave Tuffy with the new owners of their home.

"Janet will be good to Tuffy," Larry thought, "And Tuffy likes her already." Father had told him that it would be hard for Tuffy to get used to the heat in Texas and to the new surroundings. He must not think only of himself but also what was best for Tuffy.

When Father stopped the car in front of the big two story house two days later, Larry knew this must be their new home. He was anxious to look it over. "Oh boy!" he shouted when he saw the tree-house in the big tree at the corner of the yard. "This is going to be fun."

With one foot on the ladder, ready to climb up into the tree-house, he noticed a swing in another big tree. With all the excitement over the new home and all the exploring he had to do, Larry had forgotten about Tuffy - but only for a short time.

That night when Larry said his prayers, he thanked GOD for his new home and asked Him to take good care of Tuffy.

The next day Larry was sitting in his tree-house wishing Tuffy were there to keep him company. "Meow, meow." "I must be hearing things," he thought, "Tuffy is still in Idaho." He listened again. "Meow."

Quickly he scurried down the ladder and began to look around, "Meow." There, it sounded like it was coming from the wood pile. Just then he saw them - a beautiful big yellow cat with her three black and white kittens.

Larry was thrilled when the big cat rubbed against his leg affectionately. He ran to the kitchen to tell Mother about his find and to get some milk for the little family of cats.

"I'll name her Taffy," he thought as he watched her and the kittens lapping up the milk, "And I'll name all three kittens Tuffy 'cause they look just like Tuffy."

Suddenly Larry remembered The memory verse he had learned last week. Luke 6:38. "Give and it shall be given unto you, in good measure." And he knew that GOD'S promises are true. For he had given his Tuffy to Janet, now GOD had given him Taffy and three Tuffys in return.

AN ALLEGORY CHRISTMAS STORY

ON THE FIRST CHRISTMAS EVE,
  A LONG TIME AGO,
THE COLD WIND WAS BLOWING
  A PROMISE OF SNOW.

A LITTLE BOY LOST
  FROM HIS PARENTS THAT DAY,
WENT INTO THE STABLE
  TO KEEP WARM IN THE HAY.

'TWAS PAST THE MID-NIGHT
  HE AWOKE FROM HIS SLEEP,
TO THE LOWING OF CATTLE
  AND BLATTING OF SHEEP.

HE HEARD THE LOW VOICES
  OF STRANGERS NEAR-BY,
AND THE SOFT SOUND
  OF A NEW BABY CRY.

THERE IN A HAY MANGER
  NOT TEN FEET AWAY,
THE SWEET BABY JESUS
  IN SWADDLING DID LAY.

SOON THERE CAME SHEPHERDS
  AND THE WISE MEN THREE.
THE NEW SON OF GOD,
  THEY HAD COME TO SEE.

THEY BROUGHT GIFTS OF MYRRH,
  FRANKINCENSE AND GOLD,
REPEATING GOOD TIDINGS
  THE ANGELS HAD TOLD.

THE LITTLE BOY MARVELED
  AT WHAT HE HAD SEEN,
AND WONDERED WHAT GIFT
  HE COULD GIVE THE NEW KING.

HE THOUGHT AND HE THOUGHT,
  "HOW CAN I DO MY PART? -
I KNOW WHAT I'LL GIVE HIM!
  I'LL GIVE HIM MY HEART."

THIRTY YEARS LATER
  JESUS SAID, "FOLLOW ME."
AND MATTHEW THE BOY,
  WAS A MAN NOW, YOU SEE.

GLADLY HE FOLLOWED
  THE MASTER AWAY,
AND BECAME HIS DISCIPLE
  FROM THAT VERY DAY.

SUMMER FUN

WHEN SUMMER DAYS ARE HOT AND LONG,
WE PUT OUR LITTLE SWIMSUITS ON.

AND RUN BENEATH THE WATER SPRAY,
OF THE SPRINKLER HALF THE DAY.

NEIGHBOR KIDS FROM ALL ABOUT,
RUN THROUGH THE WATER WITH A SHOUT.

EVEN BABY TAKES A TURN.
IT DIDN'T TAKE HIM LONG TO LEARN.

AND WHEN THE KIDS ARE ALL PLAYED OUT,
MOM TURNS OFF THE WATERSPOUT.

PLAYING CHECKERS

I LIKE TO PLAY CHECKERS WITH GRANDPA,
FOR HE ALWAYS PLAYS WITH A GRIN,
AND HE DOESN'T SEEM TO MIND AT ALL,
THE FACT THAT I ALWAYS WIN.

THE RIGHT FOOT

I ASKED SISTER TO SHOW ME,
   WHICH SHOE WENT ON WHICH FOOT.
SHE SHOWED ME THE FIRST ONE,
   BUT I DIDN'T KNOW,
WHERE THE OTHER TO PUT.

LEMONADE STAND

"LEMONADE FOR SALE –
    LEMONADE FOR SALE,"
SAID LITTLE KALE
    AS HE STOOD BY HIS PAIL.
"A NICKLE A GLASS
    OR TWO FOR A DIME.
IT'S A HOT SUMMER DAY,
    IT'S LEMONADE TIME."

"LEMONADE FOR SALE –
    LEMONADE FOR SALE,"
AS HE SQUEEZED MORE LEMONS
    INTO THE PAIL.
A LITTLE MORE WATER,
    SUGAR AND ICE,
WITH JUST A TOUCH
    OF UNUSUAL SPICE.

"LEMONADE FOR SALE –
    LEMONADE FOR SALE,"
HE CALLED AGAIN
    AS HE DIPPED FROM HIS PAIL,
THE MAN GAVE HIM A QUARTER –
    SAID, "I'LL HAVE FIVE,"
KALE EXCLAIMED,
    "GOODNESS SAKES ALIVE!"

"LEMONADE FOR SALE –
    LEMONADE FOR SALE."
THEN TWO LITTLE LADIES
    STEPPED UP TO HIS PAIL.
THEY SAID, "WE'RE SO THIRSTY,
    WE MUST HAVE TWO."
HE WASTED NO TIME,
    HE KNEW WHAT TO DO.

"LEMONADE FOR SALE –
    LEMONADE FOR SALE."
SOON SCRAPING THE BOTTOM
    OF THE PAIL.
HIS PAIL WAS EMPTY
    BUT HE DIDN'T POUT.
HE HUNG UP A SIGN THAT READ,
    "SORRY – SOLD OUT."

BUBBLES

SEE THE PRETTY BUBBLES,
  FLOATING IN THE AIR ?
THEY LAND ON MY NOSE,
  AND LAND IN MY HAIR.

THEY FLOAT OUT THE WINDOW,
  BUT I DON'T CARE,
I'LL MAKE MORE BUBBLES
  'TIL THEY'RE EVERYWHERE.

I'LL MAKE SOME FOR BABY,
  SITTING IN HIS CHAIR,
AND SOME FOR KITTY CAT,
  TO POP IN THE AIR.

IF I GET REAL GOOD,
  I'LL BLOW BUBBLES AT THE FAIR,
IN A SHINY COSTUME,
  RIDING ON A MARE.

99

I WONDER

I WONDER HOW THE BABY CHICK,
  GOT INTO IT'S TIGHT SHELL,
AND ALWAYS SEEMS TO COME OUT FINE.
  IT'S MORE THAN I CAN TELL.

I WONDER HOW A TINY SEED,
  WHEN PLANTED IN THE GROUND,
CAN GROW INTO A TREE AS TALL,
  AS ANY TO BE FOUND.

I WONDER HOW THE HONEY BEE,
  CAN MAKE THE SWEET HONEY,
WHEN NOTHING ELSE ON EARTH CAN.
  IT SEEMS TO ME QUITE FUNNY.

I WONDER HOW THE WEE SPIDER,
  WEAVES HIS STRONG WEB SO FAIR,
TO CATCH INSECTS FOR HIS SUPPER,
  AND SWING HIMSELF THROUGH AIR,

IT IS REALLY NO GREAT WONDER,
  WHEN I STOP TO CONSIDER,
THAT WITH GOD ALL THINGS ARE POSSIBLE,
  FOR HE'S THE GREAT CREATOR.

Mark 10:27   (LUKE 1:37)

100

PRETTY IS -

PEGGY'S MOTHER ALWAYS TOLD HER,
WHAT A PRETTY GIRL SHE WAS.
THEN SHE'D ALSO SMILE AND ADD,
"PRETTY IS, AS PRETTY DOES."

PRETTY IS - SWEET AND LOVING,
PRETTY IS - THOUGHTFUL AND KIND,
PRETTY IS - ALWAYS SMILING,
PRETTY IS - WILLING TO MIND.

NOW PEGGY TELLS HER DAUGHTERS,
WHAT PRETTY LITTLE GIRLS SHE HAS.
THEN SHE ALWAYS SMILES AND SAYS,
"PRETTY IS, AS PRETTY DOES."

CHRIST IS LORD

RINGS AND THINGS

WHEN DALE WAS A TINY TOT,
    NO HIGHER THAN YOUR KNEE,
HE CLIMBED UP ON THE VANITY,
    TO SEE WHAT HE COULD SEE.

HE OPENED MOTHER'S JEWELRY BOX,
    AND MUCH TO HIS SURPRISE,
THERE WERE ALL HER RINGS AND THINGS,
    RIGHT BEFORE HIS EYES.

HE PUT HER PRETTY BRACELETS ON,
    THEN ONE NECKLACE AND ANOTHER.
THE RINGS WENT ON HIS FINGERS,
    AND - "OH, OH, HERE COMES MOTHER."

THE PEACEMAKER

From the moment Dale opened his eyes this morning, he knew it was going to be a very special day. Today was his fifth birthday and Mother had promised him a party this year. She had invited all his little friends.

All day Dale had helped Mother as much as he could. He had emptied garbage, fed the puppies, straightened his room and dusted the furniture. Almost before he knew it, it was two o'clock.

The doorbell rang and Dale ran to open the door. "Happy birthday, Dale," Todd said as he handed the pretty gift to Dale.

"Thank you," Dale said and placed the gift on the little stand by the door. "Oh, here comes Brad and Danny." Soon Kenneth and Kevin arrived with their gift and all began to play games. Mother had a funny little hat and whistle for each of them.

After several games, Mother lit the candles on the cake. Dale closed his eyes and thought for a moment, then quietly made his wish. He took a deep breath and with one blow he put out all the candles.

Mother cut the cake and served it with ice-cream. The six little boys all sat up to the dining table and bowed their heads. "Bless this food which now we take and make us good for JESUS' sake. Amen,"

Dale said, and the little boys began to eat.

At last the moment came that Dale had been waiting for all day. It was time to open the gifts. As he started to pull the paper and ribbons off the first one, Brad began to cry. Great big tears rolled down his face. "Waa! Waa! I wanna open some presents too."

At first Dale didn't know what to think, then he went over and put his arm around Brad and said, "O.K., Brad, you may help me open presents."

Brad wiped his eyes on his shirt sleeve and together the two boys opened the gifts. There was a little red truck from Todd, a book from Brad, mittens from Danny and a shirt from the twins.

"Thanks, everybody," Dale said, "Now I have a little gift for you." Quickly he ran into his room and came out with a small box. In the box were five little cars. Each a different color. "You may pick the one you want and take it home with you," he said.

After the boys had left, Dale helped Mother clean up. Mother gave Dale a big hug and said, "I am very proud of you, Dale, for letting Brad help you open the gifts so he wouldn't feel so badly. You know, Dale, JESUS once said, 'Blessed are the peacemakers: for they shall be called the children of GOD'." (Matthew 5:9)

I'M JUST A CHILD

LORD, I'M JUST A LITTLE CHILD.
 I KNOW YOU UNDERSTAND.
WHEN I'M TEMPTED TO DO WRONG,
 I NEED TO HOLD YOUR HAND.

SOMETIMES WHEN I'VE NOT BEEN GOOD,
 I COME TO YOU IN PRAYER,
AND ASK YOU TO FORGIVE ME.
 I KNOW THAT YOU WILL HEAR.

I OFTEN FEEL QUITE AFRAID,
 WHEN I'M ALONE AT NIGHT.
I TURN MY THOUGHTS TO YOU, LORD,
 THEN EVERYTHING'S ALRIGHT.

WHEN I GROW TO BE A MAN,
 I'LL WALK AND TALK WITH YOU.
I'LL PLACE MY HAND IN YOUR HAND,
 AND GO WHERE YOU WANT ME TO.

LEARNING

I LEARNED SOMETHING NEW TODAY.
I'D WORKED UNTIL I WAS BLUE,
BUT I FINALLY GOT IT RIGHT AT LAST.
I LEARNED TO TIE MY OWN SHOE.

SAM

SAM IS AN UNUSUAL PARROT.
HIS CHATTER WOULD MAKE YOUR HEAD SPIN,
AND HE SCREAMS SO LOUD WHEN STRANGERS COME,
THAT HE SCARES THEM NEAR OUT OF THEIR SKIN.